DINOSAUR

THE ESSENTIAL GUIDE

WALT DISNEY
PICTURES PRESENTS

DINOSAUR

THE ESSENTIAL GUIDE

A Dorling Kindersley Book

CONTENTS

FOREWORD

Dinosaur is a movie that transports you to a time when the most extraordinary creatures ruled the world.

Thanks to Disney's pioneering animation technology, dinosaurs will never again be confined to the realms of textbooks and the imagination. *Dinosaur* opens a window onto prehistoric life on Earth as never seen before. And the sight will take your breath away. For the first time, see the reality of a world where the plains shudder under the weight of vast iguanodon herds, where the canyons hide packs of hissing raptors, and the forests echo with the roars of the largest carnivores ever to walk the planet.

Created for the movie, the creatures appearing in this Essential Guide have the mottled skin, fleshy weight, and matted fur of real, living animals. Dorling Kindersley uses captions, annotation, and Disney's stunning, computer-generated photography to explain every character and setting with detail and clarity.

So sit back, and let this Essential Guide take you to a land where the air smells of volcanic dust and the trees of Lemur Island hide curious eyes in the dark.

Welcome to the world of *Dinosaur*.

Pam Marsden
Producer, *Dinosaur*

THE CRETACEOUS WORLD

Inside an egg, an unborn baby sees the dim glow of the world outside, filtering through the shell. Shadows move, strange and reptilian. This is the faraway light of the Cretaceous Period, the golden age of the dinosaurs. It is a world where thousands of species flourish and roam. But it is also a savage, predatory world, where life can be short, and speed and watchfulness are essential to survival. This is the story of a dinosaur that survived. This is Aladar's story.

PARADISE

In a lush green valley millions of years ago, a magnificent herd of dinosaurs grazes and rears its young. High mountains overlook the harmonious scene, and give shade during the hot afternoons. Rich foliage provides food for young and old, great and small. In a place of such fertile beauty, these vast creatures thrive.

A three-ton pachyrhinosaur ambles slowly to the watering hole, with a brachiosaur for company.

Hundreds of nesting mothers adorn the fertile plain with their eggs. All stay together in the open and keep an eye on one another's nests, in case a fast and stealthy predator should suddenly appear and steal an egg.

Welcome Watering Hole

The nesting grounds surround a large freshwater lake, used for drinking and bathing. Herd dinosaurs are highly social animals, and during the nesting season the lake is the center of their bustling community.

CRETACEOUS LIFE

• During the Cretaceous Period, flowering plants, such as auricaria, have replaced many of the seed ferns and conifers common in the Jurassic Period.

• Small mammals are multiplying fast as climates become more varied, but reptiles still dominate life on Earth.

Giant, prehistoric dragonfly

Winged lizard

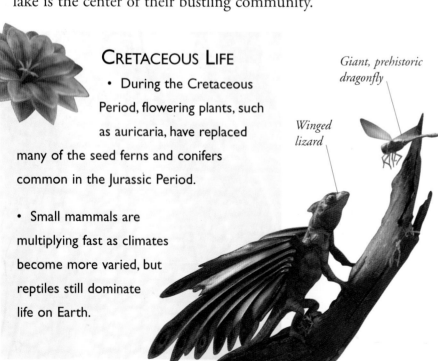

Brachiosaur   *Dense, tropical forest*   *Volcanic plateau*

Parasaurolophus   *Freshwater lake*   *Cycad tree*

Distracted by a flock of ichthyornis flying overhead, a mother does not at first notice a child parasaurolophus poking his head into the nest, looking for something to play with. When she does see him, she pushes him gently away with her nose.

THE NEST

At the edge of the herd a female iguanodon looks after her nest with maternal contentment. Her newly laid eggs are mottled with veins and color, and lie safely in a warm bed of earth and leaves. She lovingly arranges them into a neat circle and looks forward to watching them hatch.

Watchful eye

Patterned skin

Nest

Lush, fertile vegetation

Grazing iguanodons　　*Grazing ceratopsians*

Infant parasaurolophus　　*Flock of ichthyornis*　　*Grazing family of hadrosaurs*

Happy Playground

Small hadrosaur and iguanodon children scamper around the nests and through the legs of the leviathans drinking at the lake. Not every mother can keep a constant eye on where her children are when they reach such an energetic and curious age.

The little parasaurolophus has not yet learned what it means to run in fear for his life. Experience will soon teach him.

Remaining in the open gives the herd greater warning of approaching predators. The plain is ridged with a dense, dark forest best not ventured into alone.

CARNOTAURS

With its head lowered and its jaws gaping to reveal razor-sharp teeth, the sight of a charging carnotaur is a herd's worst nightmare. These huge, vicious flesh-eaters strike terror into grazing animals, who live in constant fear of attack. Carnotaurs are ambush predators, and a herd often gets no warning before the monster is in their midst.

Bull-like horn

The forest hides the hungry eyes of a gigantic carnotaur. It watches the herd and waits for the moment to attack.

Forward-facing eye

Surprise Attack

An infant parasaurolophus playing at the forest's edge disturbs a hidden carnotaur. Suddenly, with a noise of splintering branches, the monster bursts forward, and terror overcomes the herd.

Aladar's mother bravely defies the beast that tramples her nest and destroys her eggs. One day, the son she never knows will avenge her for this tragedy.

Bad breath

Serrated teeth

Massive neck

Tiny arm

A carnotaur's jaws are big enough to swallow a human whole!

CARNOTAURS

• Like other giant meat-eaters of the Cretaceous, carnotaurs have large skulls, powerful hind legs, and tiny arms, but are unusual for having distinctive "bull" horns.

• Carnotaurs hunt alone or in pairs. They often eat prey killed by smaller pack predators, like raptors.

Pachyrhinosaurs can use their fearsome horns to defend themselves against predators. For a carnotaur, a rapid, surprise attack from the rear is therefore essential.

Aim and Bite

The carnotaur does not bother with the smaller creatures it outruns. It knows that a stampede will leave behind the larger stragglers unable to hide in the herd. It attacks in a headlong rush with its mouth wide open. The resulting impact causes a rapid death to its victim.

Bony, spiked cones

Battle scars

The Fireball has driven two carnotaurs north in search of food. Their powerful sense of smell keeps them on the trail of Kron's Herd—and they are gaining rapidly, scavenging on food left by raptors along the way.

Stiff, heavy tail to aid balance

Overlapping, disc-shaped scales

As the carnotaurs close in on Aladar's cave hiding place, one of the hunters pokes its head slowly through the waterfall at the entrance. Inside, no one dares move!

Coarse underbelly

Thick, muscular calf

Finally finding its voice, the Herd stands together and corners a carnotaur. Fear sweeps over the monster at the sight of such courage, and it panics!

GORY JAWS

A carnotaur must carefully judge its attack. A mistimed lunge could give prey time to sidestep and defend itself. Once its victim is down, the carnotaur uses sharp teeth to devour the meat. The predator's jaws are flexible on both sides, and bulge sideways to let it swallow large pieces.

THE EGG THIEVES

During the carnotaur's attack, the mother's nest is destroyed. One egg remains miraculously unbroken, but alone and vulnerable. A small oviraptor, watching from the trees, sees his chance and snatches the egg from the nest. Quickly, before the mother returns, he darts into the forest, clutching his prize in his long fingers.

Egg Scramble

In the darkness of the forest, the thief stops to devour the egg alone and finds a hard rock to smash it on. But this egg is tough. It won't crack. Suddenly, another hungry oviraptor leaps in to grab it.

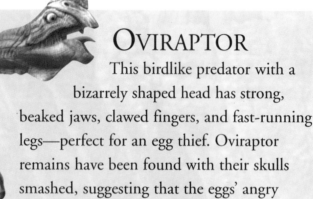

OVIRAPTOR

This birdlike predator with a bizarrely shaped head has strong, beaked jaws, clawed fingers, and fast-running legs—perfect for an egg thief. Oviraptor remains have been found with their skulls smashed, suggesting that the eggs' angry owners sometimes returned unexpectedly and caught the thieves in the act!

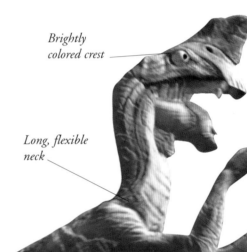

Brightly colored crest

Long, flexible neck

Long forearm

Skin patterned for camouflage

Powerful leg muscles

The two scavengers greedily fight for the egg until it slips from their grasp and plunges over a steep cliff. Angry and disappointed, they then turn on each other, clawing and scratching.

The charmed egg surfaces for a moment between two talarurus basking on the rocks. Talarurus is an armored ankylosaur with an incredible bony club at the end of its tail. One swipe of this can knock a predator off its feet!

Large eye

Danger from the Deep

Basking in the river's warm current, a large aquatic labyrinthodont spots the unusual snack heading its way. It swims up to swallow the egg, only to gag on its hard shell and spit it out.

Body lightly built for speed

Powerful leg muscles

Strongly curved claw

Splash! The egg's long fall is cushioned by the deep water of a fast-flowing river. This egg is a survivor!

The egg's perilous river voyage continues through the legs of a herd of pachyrhinosaurs having a drink. During a small skirmish for a prime position, one of these behemoths unwittingly nudges the hapless egg away, sending it into a fast current.

Dinosaur Eggs

• Most dinosaurs lay eggs in mud nests or hollows scooped in sand and covered with vegetation.

• The eggs resemble large potatoes.

• The mothers of some species stay with their eggs to protect the small hatchlings. Others bury eggs in hidden places in the forest.

• Despite parental care, many young dinosaurs fall prey to flesh-eaters before reaching adulthood.

Birdlike hind limb

Long, stiff tail

Carried away by a strong, shallow current, the egg is in danger of hitting the rocks of the river's stony bed....

PTERANODON

From the spray of the waterfall, a flock of pteranodons emerges. Their vast wings flap slowly as they hunt for fish swimming near the water's surface. Rising high on a warm air current, one of them spies a catch quite unlike her usual fishy prey. She glides low over a herd of pachyrhinosaurs and snatches the egg from the water. What a treat this will make for her hungry young!

The pteranodon uses her keen eyesight to survey the river's daily offerings. When a fish comes into view, she swoops down with devastating speed to catch it with her long beak. The fish rarely see her coming!

Victory Roll

The pteranodon flies swiftly out of the valley to the plains beyond, with the egg clasped firmly in her beak. Exhilarated by the success of her hunting expedition, she swoops daringly under the massive tail of a grazing brachiosaur!

The winged reptile is soon flying out to sea, toward a mysterious tropical island, where a thunderstorm is brewing.

MOSASAUR

Pteranodons must be watchful when flying low over deep water. This gigantic sea-dwelling mosasaur has been known to attack from the waves.

Large bony crest

Long toothless beak for scooping up fish

Small, sharply focusing eye

Wing fingers

Thin, hollow bones for lightness

At the time of the Fireball, giant pterosaurs like pteranodons are starting to surrender the air to creatures more closely related to dinosaurs—the birds. Pteranodons' delicate skin membranes are easily damaged in attacks by birds.

Breast bone

Small, compact body

This pteranodon has been fishing the same river for over 30 years. Like many of her kind, she will probably perish over or in the water while hunting.

Wing is infested with tiny parasites

PTERANODON

• The pteranodon's body weighs very little, so that she can sustain flying and soaring far out over the open sea when hunting for fish. She uses her large head crest as a rudder to steer during flight.

• Some species of pteranodon have wing spans of over 30 ft (9 m), and are among the largest of all the pterosaurs ("flying lizards"). They can live for over 40 years and mate several times during their lives.

On a rocky cliff, two of the pteranodon's young screech hungrily in their nest. Today will be a disappointment for them, as mother is about to return empty-beaked!

Thin, elastic membrane

Aerial Attack

Before she can reach her nest, the pteranodon is attacked as she flies over territory fiercely defended by a flock of squawking, pecking ichthyornis. Outnumbered, she is forced to drop the precious egg in order to fend off the feathery fighters.

Wing of skin

Four-fingered feet

As thunderclouds gather darkly, the egg falls far through the island's damp tropical air. Tumbling into the upper fronds of rainforest trees, it enters a dark, green world, and lands with a soft thump on the mossy branch of a huge tree—undamaged.

LEMUR ISLAND

In the thick, virgin forest, tropical birds shriek and chatter. Small furry creatures cascade down the trees and curious eyes sparkle in the emerald light. The egg has fallen into a world quite unlike the one it left behind. Lemur Island is a lost world. Secluded from the savagery of the Mainland, island life evolved in peace and gave rise to a colony of quick and intelligent mammals, the lemurs. Ancient folklore handed down through the generations is the only knowledge the lemurs have of the terrifying monsters that live across the sea.

PLIO

Plio steps cautiously and deliberately towards the egg, sniffing it with trepidation. It seems enormous to her—like some alien monolith fallen from the sky—and unlike anything she's ever seen.

Yar's daughter, Plio, is the clan's mother figure. She is a kind-hearted peacemaker who embodies the compassionate and loving nature of the lemurs. Her wise counsel and maternal intuition guide the community in its daily life. Plio provides a balance to Yar's worrying and eccentricity, and her good sense saves the baby Aladar.

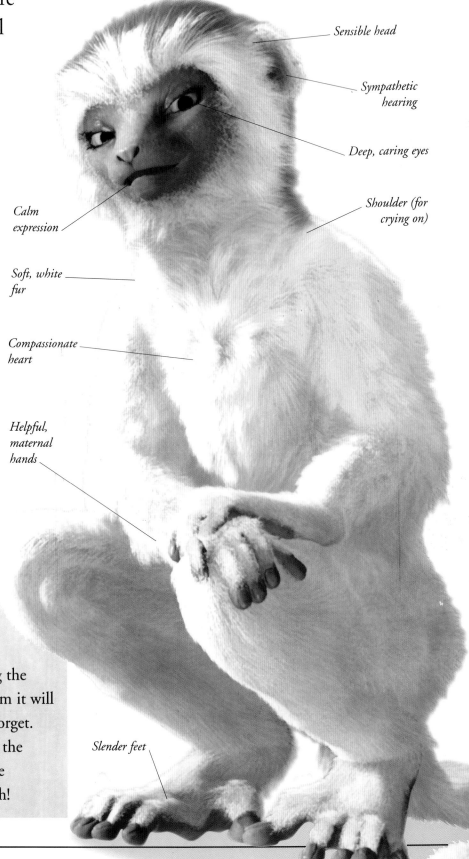

Sensible head

Sympathetic hearing

Deep, caring eyes

Shoulder (for crying on)

Calm expression

Soft, white fur

Compassionate heart

Helpful, maternal hands

Slender feet

Mother Love

Unlike Yar, Plio has no fear of the little burping baby that hatches from the shell. Her maternal instinct is to hold it and give protection. She senses in her heart that this strange infant's arrival is a good omen that will have great significance for the clan's future.

ADVISOR

Under the Ritual Tree, Plio advises the girls on how to behave toward the boys during the ceremony. She tells them it will be a day they'll never forget. She's right, but not for the reasons she thinks—the Fireball is nearing Earth!

Plio watches Aladar and Neera talk to each other under the setting sun and gently wakes her father. Her heart is full of happiness to see the boy she adopted as her son fall in love with a mate of his own. Is that a tear in the corner of Yar's eye?

In the cave, Plio takes pity on the badly injured Bruton. She picks a small spikey plant from the wall and pours its gooey liquid over the warrior's wounds, pleased to be using her nursing skills. He tries to ignore her, thinking she is giving him false hope, but he soon feels better.

Scaled Down

In her new home, Plio must get used to being one of the smallest of all the mothers. Despite being dwarfed by the dinosaurs, the nesting females hold Plio in high regard. They ask her counsel on everything from choosing a mate to dealing with difficult kids!

SURI

Innocent of life's cruelties, Plio's daughter Suri bursts with energy and happiness. She is very close to Aladar and loves the fact that she has a two-ton dinosaur for an older brother. However, her view of the world changes darkly when the island is destroyed and she has to face the terrors of the Mainland. She clings to Plio, her one source of security.

Suri tries to coax two tiny dinosaur orphans out of a pothole. They've had no water and seem scared of Suri. "Don't worry, she's just a hairball," Aladar tells them. "And proud of it!" Suri adds.

In their chasing game on Lemur Island, Suri tries escaping Aladar by racing up a tree. Too late! The gaping iguanodon mouth lunges and encloses her in midair, swallowing her whole. Not until a muffled voice cries, "Let me out!" does he spit her out, drenched in dinosaur slobber. Suri loves this game!

Downy infant hair

Bright, alert eyes

As she matures, Suri's soft brown fur will whiten, and her tail will lengthen.

Playful expression

Sensitive ears

YAR

Elder statesman of the lemur clan, Yar is officially retired, but still sticks his nose into everyone's business. His gruff, blustering manner disguises a warm heart; and despite his stubbornness, he is probably the biggest softie on the island. During the lemurs' ordeal on the Mainland, Yar keeps trying to assert his authority, but is the first to feel scared when danger approaches!

Yar paces up and down a mossy branch, scaring the kids with his prophecies about the baby dinosaur. "It's a cold-blooded monster from across the sea," he moans, theatrically. "Things like that eat things like us as snacks!"

Yar is really trying to hide his own fear, of course. The old lemur wants a quiet life in his old age and doesn't like risks!

Baby Bother

After Yar has succeeded in terrifying everybody—"One day we'll turn our backs, it'll be picking us out of its teeth!"—Plio relents, and hands him the baby to destroy. Caught off guard, but wanting to appear brave, Yar holds it out over the abyss. The little dinosaur just coos, unaware of the danger it's in. Yar can't do it. The baby smiles, and the old lemur's heart melts!

Holding the baby is a humbling experience for Yar. This surely isn't the face of a monster.

THE LOVE MASTER

Yar proudly demonstrates a few of the traditional male moves the boys should use to attract a girl at the Ritual Tree ceremony. He may be old, but "the master" still knows all the best tricks!

Yar snaps out of the happy reverie he'd fallen into during the Ritual Tree ceremony when he smells a sharp change in the air. Something ominous is definitely wafting their way. He little suspects that what is to follow will make him take risks far greater than accepting a baby dinosaur onto the island!

Yar has a soul mate companion in the grouchy Eema. They get along fine, but like to tease each other. From his perch on Eema's crest he informs the weary styracosaur that she's veering off course. "That's all I need," she says, "a monkey on my back!"

RAPTORS EVERYWHERE

On the Mainland, Yar assures the others that there's nothing to be afraid of, but then jumps out of his skin when Zini taps  him on the shoulder. There are raptors everywhere! One bites Aladar's leg, and another leaps onto his back, lunging for Yar, who is losing his grip. Plio and Zini pull him back up just in time.

Furrowed brow

Wise, friendly eyes

Statesmanlike beard

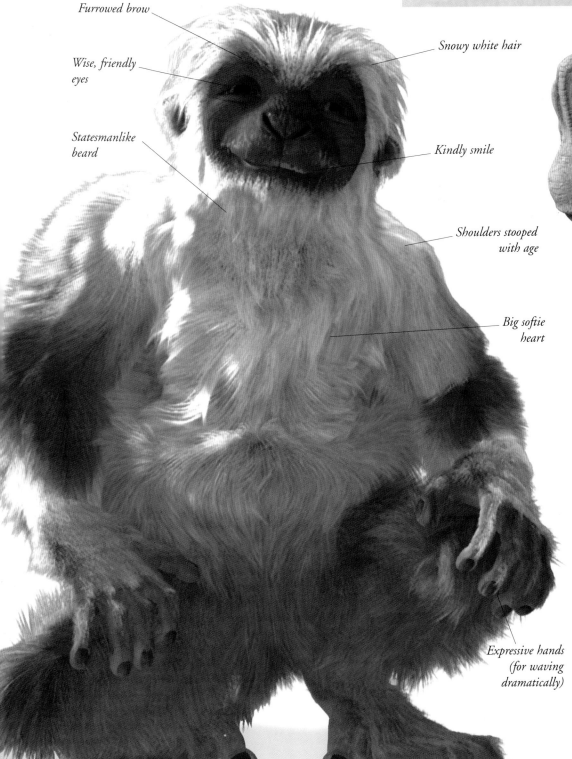

Snowy white hair

Kindly smile

Shoulders stooped with age

Big softie heart

Expressive hands (for waving dramatically)

Yar-hoo!

Yar gets a great view from the top of Baylene's head. With no trees to climb since they arrived on the Mainland, the lemurs spend a lot of time hopping up and down the brachiosaur's neck! The others get used to her immense size more quickly than Yar, who still can't quite believe she's real!

At the Nesting Grounds, Yar settles back comfortably into a grandfatherly life. Now a very happy and venerable old lemur, he looks forward to imparting his wisdom to his new great-grandson—Aladar's baby.

21

ALADAR

Secluded all his life on Lemur Island, Aladar has never met another iguanodon. When only a tiny hatchling, he is adopted by the clan of lemurs that finds him, and grows up under their loving influence to become kind, generous, and playful. As a result, Aladar is blissfully free from the outdated herd mentality of the rest of his species.

Yar can't destroy the baby Aladar when he sees its little face. The iguanodon is adopted by Plio as a son, and the story of the day an egg fell from the sky passes into lemur folklore.

The years pass and the baby becomes a handsome, two-ton teenager. Fortunately, the island is rich and fertile enough to feed his huge daily intake of leaves and fruit!

Aladar's powerful body can run fast to escape predators. In defense, he can use his arms, tail, and warlike bellow.

Spiny ridge

Forest Ambush

Foliage flies and the ground rumbles as Aladar chases his lemur brothers and sisters through the forest, shrieking with excitement. The game ends when the lemurs set an "ambush" and tickle him till he keels over. "Come on," he chuckles. "Pick on someone your own size!"

Stiff, heavy tail

Powerful hind leg

Playful, sensitive tail end

IGUANODONS

• Iguanodons are peaceful plant-eaters that can grow to 33 ft (10 m) in length and 3 tons in weight.

• They flourish in large, close-knit migratory herds that few predators dare attack.

• Their highly specialized hands have three fingers, one spike, and a vestigial toe.

The island's only iguanodon is a favorite mode of transportation for the lemurs. As a change from swinging through trees, they catch a ride on his back!

Plio comforts Aladar after the lemurs' ritual ceremony. She wishes he could meet a mate of his own someday.

EVENING OMEN

In the evening's dying light, showers of shooting stars herald the coming of the Fireball. Aladar watches in awe—he's never seen anything so lovely or unsettling. Suddenly, a feeling of dread comes over him. His carefree days are at an end and he is about to be catapulted into a world of danger and adventure.

Crest for the lemurs to hold on to

Tough, scaly skin

After the Fireball, Aladar plunges over the cliff with the lemurs on board, just as a monstrous wall of flame devours the last of the island. The waves are rising dangerously as he searches for his family.

Mottled colors

As soon as he arrives on the Mainland, Aladar comes face to face with something truly evil for the first time in his life—a pack of attacking raptors. Nothing he knew on the island ever wanted to kill him!

Flexible neck

Flaring nostrils

Charming smile

Friendly eyes

Strong, masculine hand

Sharp thumb spike

First Love

As if the shock of seeing the Herd were not enough, Aladar collides with Neera, the first female iguanodon he has ever seen. Suddenly, he feels all the pain of adolescence: attraction and rejection.

ZINI

Yar thinks the baby Aladar may become dangerous, but the infant Zini sees the dinosaur has no teeth. "What's he gonna do, gum us to death?"

Aladar's best friend is Zini, probably the clumsiest lemur of the clan. Undeterred by his own clownish appearance and accident-prone nature, Zini fancies himself a smooth operator and a ladies' lemur. Sadly, he's not quite the hit with the ladies he imagines, but this never sinks in with him. In the end, however, his courage makes him the girls' idol.

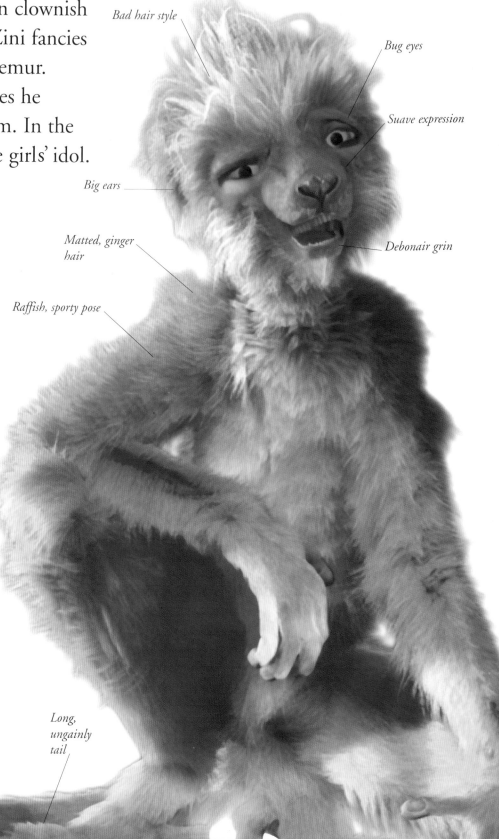

Bad hair style

Bug eyes

Suave expression

Big ears

Matted, ginger hair

Debonair grin

Raffish, sporty pose

Long, ungainly tail

The Professor of Love

Before the Ritual Tree ceremony, Aladar finds his friend on the beach rehearsing corny pickup lines. These include, "Hey, sweetie, if you'll be my bride I'll groom ya." Zini believes he's hot stuff and is completely confident he'll bowl the girls over!

Zini is very dejected when he goofs up the Ritual Tree ceremony.

Thinking he's doing Aladar a favor, Zini catcalls Neera, then hides behind his friend's head! Aladar is left dumbstruck, wearing an embarrassed smile. He can do without any more matchmaking help from the "Love Monkey"!

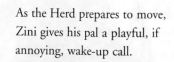

As the Herd prepares to move, Zini gives his pal a playful, if annoying, wake-up call.

LEMUR LAUGHS

Zini keeps his family's spirits up during the Herd's grueling march by always looking on the bright side. He doesn't even take Bruton seriously—"Sheez, is that guy ugly or what?"—and sees the whole ordeal as an opportunity for finding his pal a girl. But as Aladar and Neera fall in love, Zini fears he'll be a lonely bachelor.

Yar occasionally finds Zini's point of view exasperating, believing the uncouth young lemur has a lot to learn. Zini, however, thinks he can learn nothing new from the advice of an old monkey!

When Baylene's huge foot sinks into the dry lake bed, Zini and Aladar start to dig around it. In his excitement at finding water, Zini falls into the hole. He tells Baylene he always did like big girls!

Just when it seems as it the cave is at a dead end, Zini smells fresh air. A chink of light appears. The Nesting Grounds!

The Surf Monkey

As the lemurs gaze in wonder at their new home, Zini is thrilled that it comes with a pool! He climbs to the top of Baylene's head as she steps delicately into the lake, then bellyflops in. Suddenly, with a cry of "Look out below!", Baylene plunges, and a huge wave sweeps Zini up like a surfer! At last he's done something cool.

Fan Club

At the Nesting Grounds, Zini is a hero, and finds himself surrounded by his new neighbors—smitten lemur girls, vying for his attention. When he asks if they'd like a game of "monkey in the middle," they mob him!

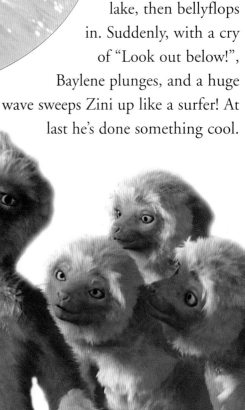

THE RITUAL TREE

High on a clifftop overlooking the ocean stands the lemurs' magnificent Ritual Tree. Every year, young lemur couples climb its ancient vines in a playful ceremony to choose a mate. This has gone on for as long as any lemur can remember. None suspects that this year's rite will be the last.

The lemurs believe that the majestic tree is sacred and has powerful hidden energies.

Ominous sunset

The lemur boys

The grove trees

Aladar

Yar wisely advises the nervous boys of the tried and tested ways to get a girl.

The Elders' Advice

Each girl carries a flower as a gift for her chosen mate. Plio warns the girls not to chase the first boy with a cute back flip and to keep them guessing. Yar tells the boys that if a cute back flip doesn't work, guess!

Grassy clearing

Aladar enters the grove in front of the Ritual Tree with the boys riding on his back. He parades them splendidly in front of the girls, who remain coy and aloof, just as Plio instructed them.

Aladar watches with a mixture of joy and sadness; he knows he will never find a mate on the island.

LEMURS

- The lemurs stay with their chosen mates for life and remain faithful.

- They feed mainly on flowers, fruit, and insects.

- The lemurs are tree-dwellers and are not very active at night.

Bathed in the glorious evening light, the girls watch with flowers in their mouths as the boys somersault and show off.

Thick leaves

Hanging vines

Still Single

Only Zini has been left behind, tangled in a vine. His feelings are hurt; but as always, he makes a joke of it. "Hey, I'm lucky to be rid of them. With the ladies, before you know it, they all want to move to a bigger tree!"

Ancient, gnarled trunk

TWO BY TWO

The boys leap for the Ritual Tree with amazing agility. Soon, the girls get caught up in the excitement and climb the vines. Then, two by two, the lemurs pair off, basking in the dual glow of love and sunset. Yar feels quite emotional, even though he's watched this ceremony countless times.

Chalky cliff edge

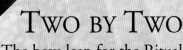

EARTH SHOCK

From the day it was born, the Earth has
been bombarded with chunks of rock and
iron from outer space. Most of these missiles
burn up in the atmosphere or are too small to
cause any harm. But every hundred million
years or so, there comes one so immense that
its impact shatters nature's delicate balance
and changes the face of the world. The life
that remains must struggle to start again.
Only the most adaptable of creatures will
survive such a catastrophe....

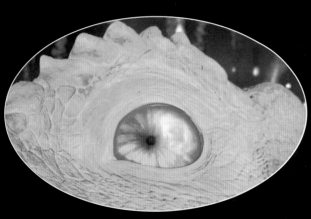

The Fireball pours out of the sky with an explosive roar. Its burning tail sears the air.

Air in front of the comet is compressed and heated.

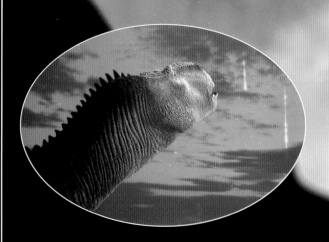

Aladar sees strange shooting stars falling to Earth, like the dying light of fireworks.

Comet becomes fiery as it enters the atmosphere.

THE FIREBALL

As the sun sets over Lemur Island, a ghostly stillness fills the air. Brilliant lights cascade across the sky. These are the advance scouts of a giant comet set on a catastrophic collision course with the Earth. Aladar and the lemurs watch in horror as it enters the sky and roars into the distance. Its impact splits the horizon like a nuclear explosion, and the blast turns night into day.

High pressure gases jet out from the core.

Massive piece of interplanetary debris.

The newly paired lemur boys and girls watch dumbstruck as the disaster unfolds overhead. None survives to enjoy their new lives together.

DANGER IN THE AIR

Even before the shooting stars appear, the lemurs' keen hearing and sense of smell alert them immediately to the impending airborne disaster. Plio has never known the island fall so eerily silent, or the air become so heavy, as if before a thunderstorm. She and Yar have a bad feeling about this....

As rapidly as it appears, the Fireball vanishes over the horizon, which suddenly flares blindingly white. Aladar is gripped by a sense of urgency.

THE COMET'S COLLISION

• The Fireball is a huge comet made of rock, iron, and ice, which travels through space at a speed of thousands of miles per hour.

• Its impact causes an explosion equal to that of several thousand nuclear bombs. A hole is punched into the Earth's crust, and the blast sends massive, high-temperature shock waves in all directions.

Tidal Wave of Fire

As the Fireball's impact sends a tidal wave of flame toward Lemur Island, thousands of fiery rocks start raining down like exploding shells. With the lemurs on his back, Aladar runs for his life through this minefield, with the falling debris pulverizing the ground all around him.

Losing ground to the wave of fire behind him, Aladar reaches a sheer cliff edge. There's no time to think —he plunges headlong into the sea!

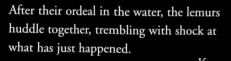

After their ordeal in the water, the lemurs huddle together, trembling with shock at what has just happened.

Yar   *Plio*

Zini   *Suri*

Aladar and the lemurs stagger ashore on a devastated beach. Evidence of the Fireball is everywhere. It is a wasteland of cinders, ash, and smoke. The lemurs look back tearfully at their island paradise, which is now a burning wilderness.

RAPTOR ATTACK

T he flesh-eating raptors have also been hit hard by the Fireball. The plentiful animals they once preyed upon have been wiped out. Now they are forced to stray far beyond their usual hunting grounds and follow Kron's Herd, waiting to attack the stragglers and the sick. To their surprise, a lone dinosaur strays straight into their pack.

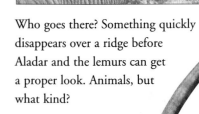

Who goes there? Something quickly disappears over a ridge before Aladar and the lemurs can get a proper look. Animals, but what kind?

Body lightly built for speed

Strongly stiffened tail

Clawed Tormentors

At first the raptors taunt Aladar, testing his strength and speed. Despite his courage, Aladar stands little chance against a large pack. Luckily, the raptors retreat when they see the oncoming Herd.

Muscular thigh

FAST KILLERS

Unlike the giant carnotaurs, speedy raptors are lightly built, and have strong arms. They are intelligent, possessing large brains, and are equipped with a devastating array of razor-sharp teeth. When running, raptors can swerve very quickly and still keep their balance, by using their long, stiffened tails as "rudders".

Sickle-shaped claw

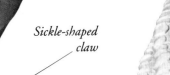

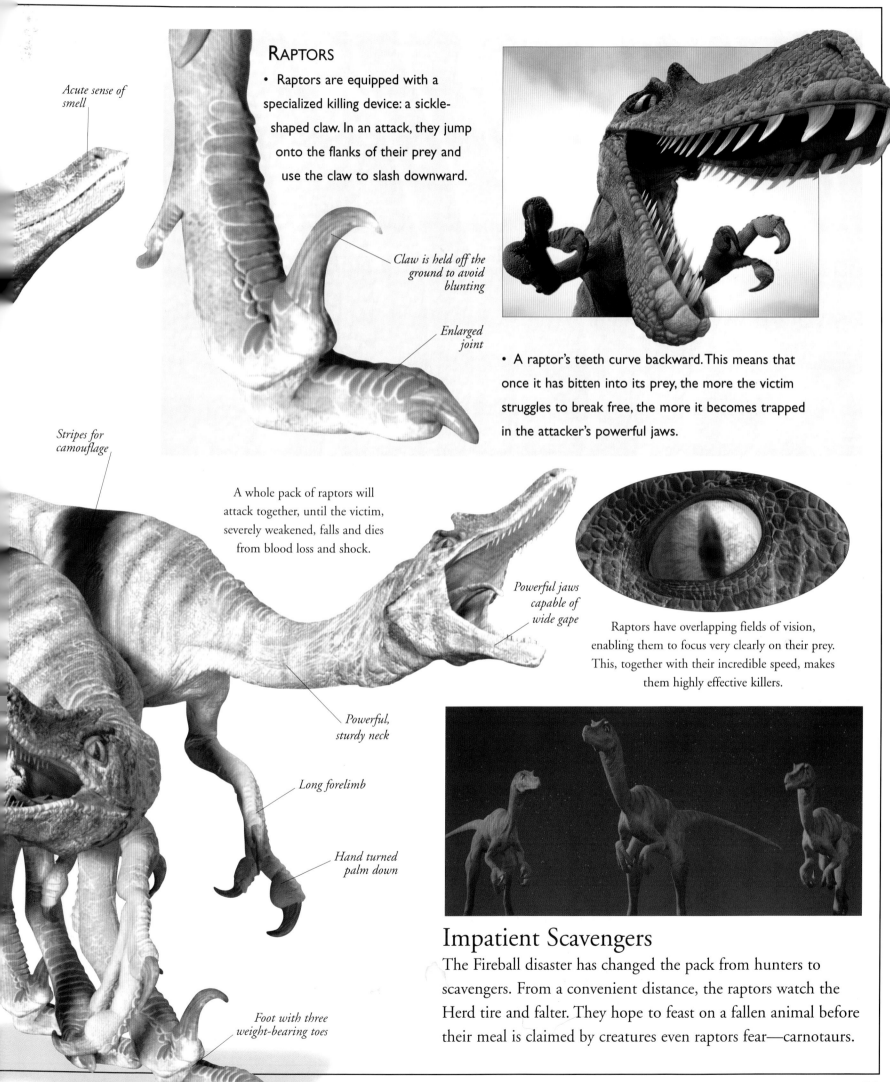

RAPTORS

- Raptors are equipped with a specialized killing device: a sickle-shaped claw. In an attack, they jump onto the flanks of their prey and use the claw to slash downward.

Acute sense of smell

Claw is held off the ground to avoid blunting

Enlarged joint

- A raptor's teeth curve backward. This means that once it has bitten into its prey, the more the victim struggles to break free, the more it becomes trapped in the attacker's powerful jaws.

Stripes for camouflage

A whole pack of raptors will attack together, until the victim, severely weakened, falls and dies from blood loss and shock.

Powerful jaws capable of wide gape

Raptors have overlapping fields of vision, enabling them to focus very clearly on their prey. This, together with their incredible speed, makes them highly effective killers.

Powerful, sturdy neck

Long forelimb

Hand turned palm down

Foot with three weight-bearing toes

Impatient Scavengers

The Fireball disaster has changed the pack from hunters to scavengers. From a convenient distance, the raptors watch the Herd tire and falter. They hope to feast on a fallen animal before their meal is claimed by creatures even raptors fear—carnotaurs.

THE HERD

Every year, a large dinosaur herd migrates to the Nesting Grounds. Dozens of different species follow the iguanodons, the Herd's leaders, on the long walk north. But this year, the Fireball has destroyed the pastures and lakes along the route, turning the formerly relaxed journey into a death march. Many will not make it.

The Herd's leader is Kron, a pitiless iguanodon. At first, the Fireball emergency strengthens his personal power over his followers.

Hunger and thirst quickly brutalize the Herd. Influenced by Kron's selfish example, no one helps the two orphans when they fall, until Neera takes pity on them.

Dawn Yawn

Aladar camps down for the night with his new friends, Baylene and Eema. Kron is puzzled by this newcomer who doesn't claim a privileged sleeping spot uphill with the other "youngbloods." At dawn, Bruton gives the signal to move, and the unhappy Herd gets wearily to its feet.

RAPTOR SNACK

A stygimoloch falls, exhausted. No one helps. Kron is willing to abandon the fallen to the mercy of the pursuing raptors. Left to its fate, this animal will be lucky if it dies before the meat-eaters find it.

From a high ridge, the Herd stares in shocked silence at the sunbaked rocks of a dry lake bed. No water, just the bones of a dead dinosaur.

Dry, cracked lake bed

Baylene

Skeleton of a ceratopsian

Kron

LONG MARCH

The Herd moves like a defeated army across an endless scorching wasteland. In previous years, the trip to the Nesting Grounds was a leisurely, social affair. There were a number of stops for grazing and bathing, before arriving in plenty of time to nest and lay eggs.

When he finds the valley entrance blocked, Kron loses his grip on reality and desperately tries to assert his power. But the Herd can see that his order to climb the rocks would be suicide. The mood is ripe for a new leader.

The Nesting Grounds have a strong healing effect on the Herd. The desperate, selfish behavior that pervaded the journey melts away, and the animals return to their natural, peaceful selves.

Child parasaurolophus

Pachyrhinosaur

Iguanodon

Child iguanodon

Microceratops

Parasaurolophus

HERD HIERARCHY

• Except for Baylene, the biggest animal in the Herd is parasaurolophus. The smallest is microceratops, which belongs to the same dinosaur family as Eema, the ceratopsians ("horned faces").

• Intelligence and agility make the iguanodons the Herd's natural leaders. Some other members aren't so gifted— beneath its thick skull, stygimoloch has a tiny brain!

Stygimoloch

Struthiomimus

Styracosaur

EEMA

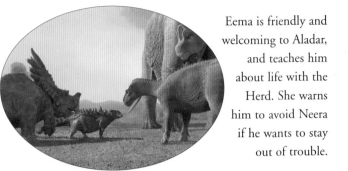

Eema is friendly and welcoming to Aladar, and teaches him about life with the Herd. She warns him to avoid Neera if he wants to stay out of trouble.

A hundred-year-old styracosaur who has been with the Herd for as long as she can remember, Eema is slow on her feet but has a quick wit. Although warm and good-natured, she has a definite attitude toward anyone who challenges her experience!

Eema regards the lemurs as extended family. She is often playfully rude to Yar, calling him "Pops," but allows him to sit on her crest and navigate!

Crusty, knobbly bump

Bony ridge

Neck frill

Bony frill spike

Broken horn

Grouchy expression

Big heart

Short, stumpy legs

QUIRKY COUPLE

Eema keeps an eye on her genteel traveling companion Baylene, who has never migrated with the Herd before. Although they are temperamentally different, Eema's gutsy tough talk is a good counterbalance to Baylene's well-bred manner, and the two old dinosaurs have become firm friends.

Fallen Lady

When the dismayed Herd discovers the lake is dry, Eema can take no more. Delirious and disoriented, she begins to roll around in the dust, as if up to her eyes in water. Aladar, deeply worried, tries to push her to her feet but fears she has simply given up. "Oh, Eema, please," says Baylene, desperately. "The Herd won't wait."

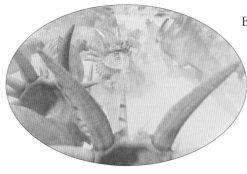

Eema is nearly killed when the Herd mobs the pool where she is drinking. She is saved by Aladar, who shields her from the violent scramble and guides her carefully out of the crowd.

Rhinoceros-like body

Hind limb

Short tail

Nails

When Eema sees the valley entrance blocked, she knows Aladar too well to stop him leaving to find the Herd. "I hope Kron's in a listening mood," she says.

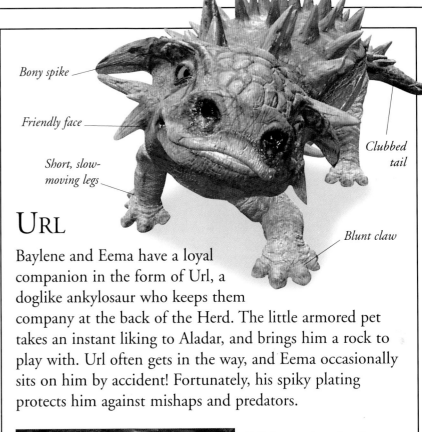

Bony spike

Friendly face

Short, slow-moving legs

Clubbed tail

Blunt claw

Url

Baylene and Eema have a loyal companion in the form of Url, a doglike ankylosaur who keeps them company at the back of the Herd. The little armored pet takes an instant liking to Aladar, and brings him a rock to play with. Url often gets in the way, and Eema occasionally sits on him by accident! Fortunately, his spiky plating protects him against mishaps and predators.

Url's interest in stalagmite-collecting pays off when he discovers a cave for the friends to hide in during a storm.

The little ankylosaur is very excited to be at the Nesting Grounds, and runs along the highway of flattened grass made by Baylene in her race for the lake!

Merry Midwife

Finally, Eema shows her supreme value to the Herd by being a loving midwife for the hatching eggs. Overcome with joy as the babies emerge, the old styracosaur bellows as loudly as she can, setting off a chorus of cheers throughout the valley. The air is filled with celebration and happiness.

BAYLENE

A brachiosaur from a bygone age, Baylene is an elegant old lady and the last of her kind. In her day, she was an aristocrat among the giant sauropods that graced the plains. But the Fireball has now forced her into the brutal migration of the Herd, an ordeal she's never experienced before. Despite her huge size, Baylene is timid and ill-prepared to survive the journey. Luckily, she's got Eema to look after her.

Along with Eema, Baylene is one of the few friendly faces to welcome Aladar and the lemurs into the savage convoy. Until Aladar gives her a reason to believe in herself, she has a low opinion of her value to the Herd, thinking she's nothing but an old fool who slows the others down.

Baylene lags painfully behind the Herd. She has never had to hurry in her life, and finds the forced pace "positively indecent" for an older lady like herself.

Nostril

Careworn eye

Gentle expression

Heavy long neck supported by large ribbed vertebrae

LATE LEARNER

Baylene would not have survived her introduction to Herd life if it hadn't been for Eema—another old lady, but far more herd-wise. The brachiosaur's refined upbringing protected her from life's meanness and she now depends on Eema's know-how to get by.

Past meets Future

Baylene smells the lemurs before she sees them on Aladar's back. At first she mistakes them for an unfortunate blemish! Their meeting is significant. The brachiosaurs' days are numbered, but the mammals' future lies ahead.

Without Baylene's mighty bulk, the friends would never have made it to the Nesting Grounds. Relying on nothing but brute force and a will to live, she pounds against the cave's blocked exit and the stones begin to fall. Baylene's head emerges from the dust. And her jaw drops at the amazing sight before her.

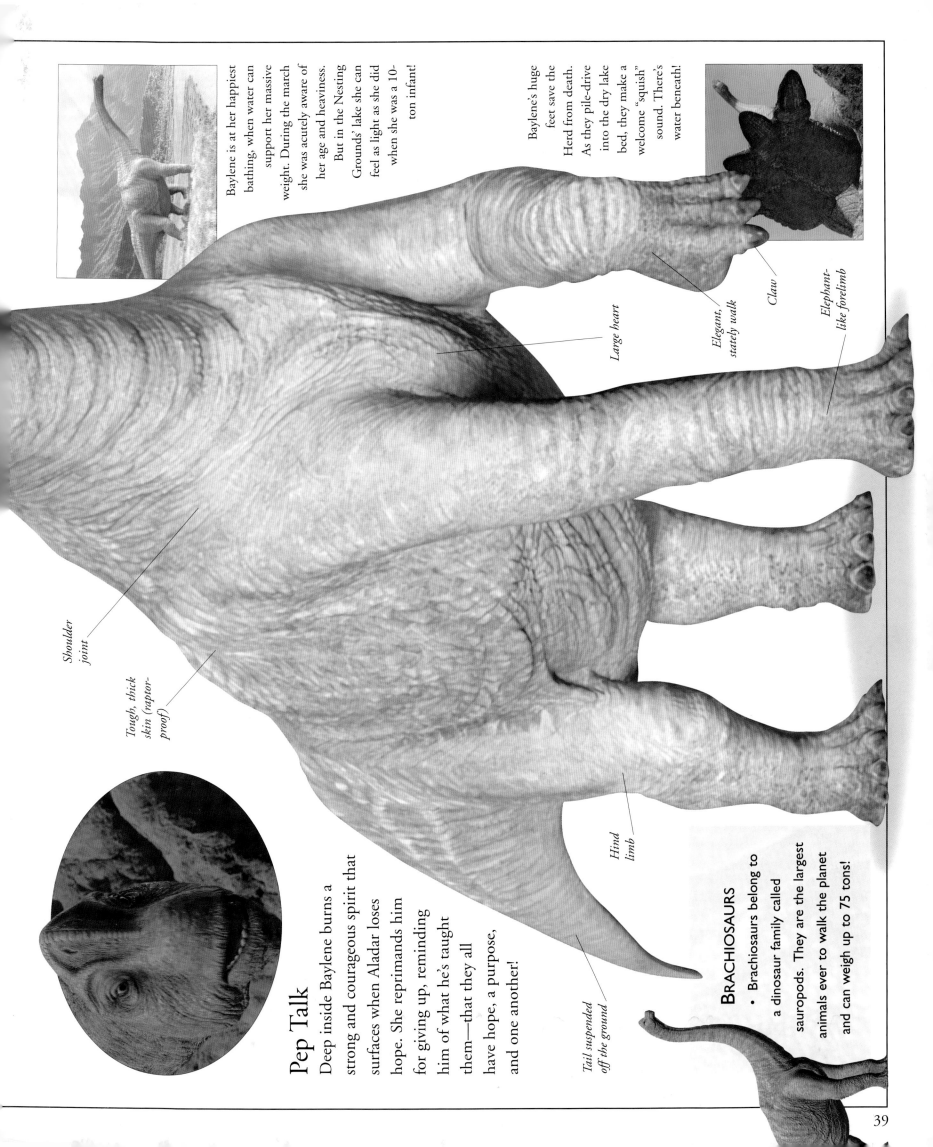

Baylene is at her happiest bathing, when water can support her massive weight. During the march she was acutely aware of her age and heaviness. But in the Nesting Grounds' lake she can feel as light as she did when she was a 10-ton infant!

Baylene's huge feet save the Herd from death. As they pile-drive into the dry lake bed, they make a welcome "squish" sound. There's water beneath!

Large heart

Elegant, stately walk

Claw

Elephant-like forelimb

Shoulder joint

Tough, thick skin (raptor-proof)

Hind limb

Pep Talk

Deep inside Baylene burns a strong and courageous spirit that surfaces when Aladar loses hope. She reprimands him for giving up, reminding him of what he's taught them—that they all have hope, a purpose, and one another!

Tail suspended off the ground

BRACHIOSAURS

• Brachiosaurs belong to a dinosaur family called sauropods. They are the largest animals ever to walk the planet and can weigh up to 75 tons!

KRON

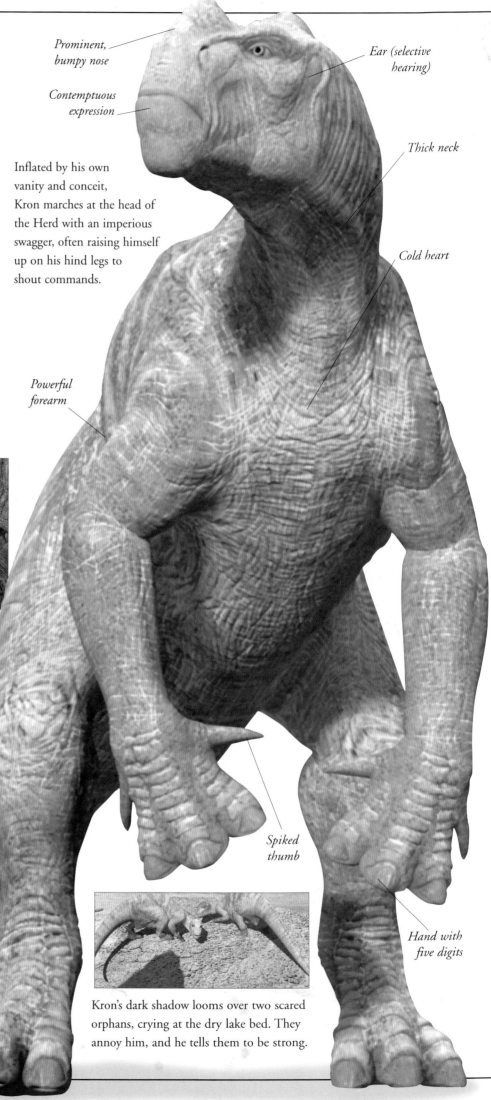

The Herd is led unmercifully by Kron, an arrogant and ruthless iguanodon. Now that the Fireball has changed the traditional route to the Nesting Grounds, Kron's old style of rule can't withstand the ever-increasing challenges of the journey—or the arrival of a far more compassionate and dynamic leader: Aladar. The tyrant soon starts to hate the young outsider.

Prominent, bumpy nose

Contemptuous expression

Ear (selective hearing)

Thick neck

Cold heart

Inflated by his own vanity and conceit, Kron marches at the head of the Herd with an imperious swagger, often raising himself up on his hind legs to shout commands.

Powerful forearm

"Watch Yourself, Boy"

Kron can't believe his ears when Aladar asks him to slow down for Baylene and Eema, who have difficulty keeping up. Not used to being questioned, Kron responds with sarcasm. "Let the weak set the pace. Now there's an idea!"

Kron watches the exhausted animals sleep. He doesn't care that the pace will lose half the Herd. He'll save those who deserve to live!

Spiked thumb

Kron usually reacts to anyone who upsets him with a heavy blow from his tail!

Heavy, stiff tail

Hooflike nails

Kron's dark shadow looms over two scared orphans, crying at the dry lake bed. They annoy him, and he tells them to be strong.

Hand with five digits

Raging Thirst

When Aladar discovers water under the dry lake bed, Kron strides over and orders everyone out of the way. Selfishly, he refreshes himself before any of his thirsting followers. He is also secretly furious that this is Aladar's discovery and not his own. Such a miraculous find would have enhanced his power over the Herd.

When Aladar realizes that Kron is about to sacrifice the stragglers to the carnotaurs, he tries to address the Herd. But before he can speak his mind, the tyrant lashes at him savagely and knocks him down. "If you ever interfere again, I'll kill you," Kron hisses.

LEADER

Kron demands absolute loyalty from his followers as he leads them on a path that seems to go nowhere. He rules through fear and offers no words of encouragement. The strong survive, and the weak should be left to their fate. To Kron's mind, anyone who questions this age-old rule is directly challenging him personally.

Faced with a landslide that blocks the entry to the Nesting Grounds, the Herd ignores Kron's insane order to start climbing. To his horror, they turn to follow Aladar and Neera. The tyrant self-righteously begins to climb alone.

Death of a Tyrant

Kron, realizing his fate

Kron is confident the animals will regret following their new leader and return to him and the old ways of the Herd. But, in fact, his refusal to embrace a new idea like "everyone counts" leads to his death. Instead of standing in solidarity with the Herd, he is left exposed like one of the stragglers he despises, and is killed by a carnotaur.

Deadly headlong rush

Rocky outcrop

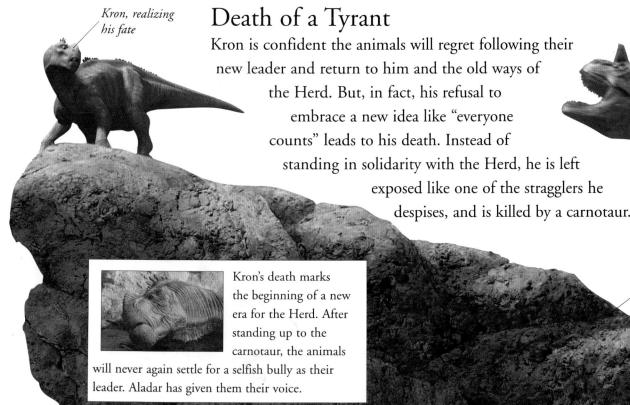

Kron's death marks the beginning of a new era for the Herd. After standing up to the carnotaur, the animals will never again settle for a selfish bully as their leader. Aladar has given them their voice.

THE ODYSSEY

The Herd obeys Kron's commands without question and is driven mercilessly across the desert by his survival-of-the-strongest mentality. Within the Herd's ranks are found both safety and death. It protects against the stalking predators with its sheer numbers, but kills with its heartless disregard for the slow and the weak. In the year of the Fireball, Kron's traditional ways are sorely tested, for few can survive the epic journey without rest and water.

NEERA

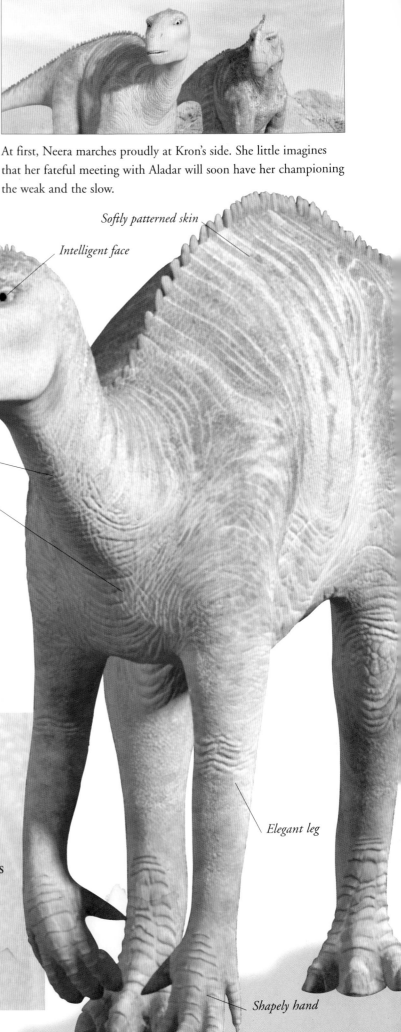

K ron's younger sister, Neera, is a beautiful, no-nonsense girl. Although as intelligent as her brother, she has a greater capacity for courage and compassion. The old ways she shares with him are challenged when she meets Aladar, whose strange ideas intrigue her.

At first, Neera marches proudly at Kron's side. She little imagines that her fateful meeting with Aladar will soon have her championing the weak and the slow.

Softly patterned skin

Intelligent face

Thoughtful expression

Slender neck

Warm heart

When Neera sees Aladar protecting Eema at the lake bed, she realizes that her idea of him as a "jerkasaurus" is unfair.

Elegant leg

Shapely hand

Bumpy Start

Neera's introduction to Aladar is an awkward one, as he bumps right into her when the Herd marches past. She simply snorts with disgust and pushes right past him, before Bruton rudely shoves him to the back.

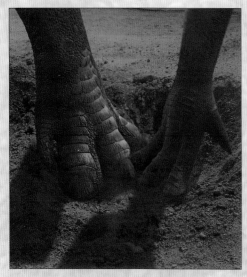

NEERA ENOUGH

Even Zini, "a couple of species removed" from Aladar, can see Neera's appeal, and knows that scaly skin, yellow eyes, and big ankles are exactly what his pal is looking for in a girl! As Aladar shows her how to find water, their hands touch, and they fall in love under a magical evening sky.

Brave New Ideal

Aladar's revolutionary idea that everyone counts triggers a full-scale transformation in Neera. This eventually leads to a heart-wrenching decision to defy her angry brother and follow the young outsider.

As one of the orphaned infants falls from exhaustion, Neera helps him up, and promises him that no one else will be left behind.

Graceful tail

Kron is immediately aware of Aladar's attraction to Neera and separates them violently.

IGUANODON INFANTS

- Iguanodons keep their young in the center of the herd, surrounded by adults, in order to protect them against stalking predators.

- Infants are able to run on two legs, although by adulthood they will move almost permanently on all fours.

- Iguanodons' large size means they must eat a lot. This is essential for infants, who will reach a weight of one to two tons in only a few short years.

After a terrible fight, Kron is poised to kill Aladar. But before the tyrant can deliver the death blow, Neera broadsides him, knocking him to the ground before a stunned Herd. She barely has time to think about what she's done when a carnotaur enters the canyon and there's a new danger to confront.

When Kron's arrogance leads to his own death, Neera is filled with a mixture of remorse and relief. She has failed to save him from himself, but she has helped to save the Herd.

At the Nesting Grouds, Neera lays her eggs and watches with Aladar, the proud father, as they hatch. Both are deeply content. Everything they have wished for has come to pass. They have fulfilled their quest and ensured the survival of their species.

BRUTON

Kron's lieutenant, Bruton, is a battle-hardened veteran of many long marches. Proud and loyal, he dutifully follows the traditional ways of the Herd. Initially mistrustful of Aladar's ragtag group of lemurs and "misfit" friends, Bruton is eventually transformed by their kindness and gives his life for Aladar.

Kron relies on his lieutenant to carry out all manner of dangerous and underhand tasks, knowing that he will obey without question. But as the journey becomes ever more desperate, even Bruton doubts the wisdom of Kron's increasingly deranged commands.

Tough, scarred hide

Crusted, bony nose

Cynical eye

Battle scar

Bulging thigh muscles

Very heavy, powerful tail

Brave heart

Bruton announces to the Herd that there's no water until they get to the other side of the desert. "And you better keep up. Because if a predator catches you, you're on your own. Move out!"

FIERCE ONE

Kron chose Bruton as his right-hand dinosaur because of his powerfully built body and fierce attitude. Bruton is a warrior who has no time for weaklings and laggards. And especially not sassy newcomers who question Kron's style! Bruton is at first very dismissive of Aladar, thinking him naive and stupid.

When Zini makes a joking remark—from the safety of his hiding place behind Aladar's head—Bruton loses his temper. "Unless you got a death wish, you and that little parasite better get moving!"

Carnotaurs' Canyon

At dusk, Bruton and his scouts are ambushed in a dark canyon. Carnotaurs lunge from the shadows. One drags off a scout, and another confronts Bruton...

Badly wounded, Bruton escapes to warn Kron of the danger ahead. A blood-curdling roar is heard—too close for comfort. The leader is furious. "You led them right to us," he hisses. "Maybe you can feed them with your hide!"

Abandoned by Kron, Bruton reluctantly joins Baylene, Eema, and the lemurs in the shelter of a cave. Aladar welcomes him, and Plio soothes his wounds with a healing plant. Bruton is confused. Why are they so kind to him?

Fate or Choice?

When Kron leaves his loyal lieutenant to the carnotaurs, Bruton's eyes are opened to his master's evil. He believes his fate is to die in the cave, but Plio tells him that's his choice, not his fate. Suddenly, he realizes what hope and courage Aladar has given these "losers" from the back of the Herd.

Blood-curdling roar

Cruel, gleeful expression

Slow, menacing advance

ENEMY AT THE GATE

The storm is getting worse. Outside the cave, two carnotaurs are silhouetted against the entrance by a lightning flash. They are sniffing the air, unsure of what's inside. Another flash reveals Aladar, and the monsters charge, chomping down on his tail!

Second carnotaur

First carnotaur

Bruton, approaching defiantly

Bruton saves Aladar and the others by ramming the monsters and holding them off while the friends escape into the cave. He fights valiantly but the carnotaurs are too big. Spotting a fragile-looking pillar, he throws himself against it and brings the roof down on the beasts. Bruton, Aladar's brave, unexpected ally, dies a hero's death.

EVERYONE COUNTS!

Aladar comes of age during the Herd's ordeal. After a quiet early life on the island, the Fireball throws him into an adventure that ignites his compassion and heroism. Aladar's charisma and belief that everyone counts finally gives the Herd such a powerful lease on life that the unimaginable happens – together they defeat a carnotaur and reject Kron!

When the Herd finds a dry lake bed, Aladar realizes that moving on at an even quicker pace is not the solution to the crisis.

Rescuer

The Herd rushes forward in a mad stampede when it hears of the water. "Wait! there's enough for everyone," Aladar shouts. No one listens. Eema is pushed and shoved but is too weak to move. Aladar has to fight his way through to reach her. His heroism is not lost on Neera.

Aladar knows that without the help of Baylene, the slowest member of the Herd, they would not have found water.

CHALLENGER

As an outsider, Aladar has never been subject to the Herd's ancient rules, and can see what's wrong with Kron's regime. The young iguanodon knows they have a better chance of surviving if everyone helps one another —not if the strong selfishly look out for themselves.

Neera is puzzled that Aladar helped Eema at the lake. "What else could we do? Leave her behind?" he asks. She tells him no one survives if they're not strong enough. "Is that you talking or your brother?" he wonders. Neera wants to believe in him. She feels confused and her loyalty to Kron is shaken.

Aladar shows the children that by working together with a little team spirit, they can make a pool of water big enough for all to share, and the smallest won't get edged out.

After the Fireball, Kron is incapable of adapting to the changed world, and reacts angrily to anyone who questions him.

Aladar bellows ferociously as he runs forward to meet the carnotaur. The effect is surprising enough to catch the monster off guard.

Spines are tense and upright

Aladar's most fierce face

CHARGE!

Faced with a huge, charging carnotaur, Aladar doesn't flee, but goes against millions of years of evolved herd instinct by running to confront the predator head on!

Bewildered, frightened expression

Hero in Despair

Despite keeping his friends going with hope, Aladar himself despairs completely in his darkest hour. Just as they find an exit to the cave, rocks fall and block it. Something in Aladar snaps and he slumps down in defeat, saying they're not meant to survive. Baylene is shocked, and tells him so. Is he really saying this? Aladar inspired them! He taught them they were all needed...

Brave, fast-beating heart

Fingers extended aggressively

Baylene is right, and with the help of Aladar and the others smashes her way through to the valley. As Aladar runs to tell the Herd, he has to hide quickly when the surviving carnotaur passes by.

The Herd enter the Nesting Grounds as transformed animals. Aladar has given them the tools to survive the future—an enthusiastic belief in themselves and a strong sense of equality. The Fireball has truly changed the world. The old order is gone and a new era of compassion is dawning.

Pounding hoof

THE BATTLE

Aladar is not afraid. He knows the carnotaur expects animals to run from it in terror. He has an idea that simply defying the beast will confuse it. And may even give it a taste of something new—fear!

As the Herd follows Aladar out of the canyon, a terrifying roar stops them all in their tracks. Blocking their way is a furious, wounded carnotaur. Its jaws gape gigantically as it steps toward the trapped animals. Blinded by fear, the Herd turns to scramble up the landslide after Kron. Aladar implores them all to make a stand and not to move. Then the beast charges....

Wounds caused during fight with Bruton

Ugly, bony spikes

Coarse red skin

Large, heavy head

Evil, yellow eye

Jaws bulge outward when swallowing

Horrible, drooling mouth

Empty stomach

This carnotaur was wounded in the cave when it attacked Bruton. Its companion was less fortunate and was killed outright when the cave roof fell in.

Thick ankles support huge weight

Instead of fleeing, Aladar rushes toward the predator, and bellows in his loudest, most aggressive voice. The carnotaur begins to slow down, clearly puzzled.

The Heroic Herd

Suddenly Neera joins Aladar before the carnotaur. Then another Herd member does the same. And another. And another. Now the carnotaur stops, bewildered. It has never seen anything like this before. Excited, the whole Herd closes ranks, unites, and bellows in deafening unison!

Cornered by the Herd, the carnotaur surveys the scene, frightened. And that's when it spots Kron...separated and alone. It sets off after him.

DOWNFALL

Kron has turned his back on the Herd he thinks no longer deserves him, and climbs the rocks alone. Finally, he turns and sees, in disbelief, the carnotaur—right behind him. Kron presses on, but reaches a cliff edge impossible to cross. He realizes his fate. The fight is brutal, and Kron dies.

The carnotaur uses Aladar's own trick against him when it floors him with a blow from the tail. Aladar winces as he lands on his chest injury.

Evil End

Neera rushes up the landslide in an attempt to save her brother. The carnotaur nearly kills her too, but Aladar reaches the scene just in time and smashes the beast in its face with a vicious tail swipe. The monster fights back, enraged, and Aladar falls down.

Aladar has defied this bully once, and he'll do it again. He gets up and rams the carnotaur toward the cliff edge. The ground gives way and the beast falls howling to its death.

DINOSAUR DEFENSE

• The iguanodons' large, daggerlike thumb spike is a very effective defense weapon. It can puncture the toughest skin.

• Many dinosaurs use their long, heavy tails in self-defense. Brachiosaurs like Baylene can flatten an attacker with a blow from a tail so long it can be hard to dodge!

Thumb spike

Noisy, brave bellow

Throat distended for loudest sound

Aladar spreads courage through the Herd like the carnotaur spreads fear. Aladar has never known the collective panic of a carnotaur attack.

Thumb spike at the ready

Tail held out stiffly

Legs pushing body forward for aggressive stance

Bull-like pawing of ground

THE NESTING GROUNDS

Hidden behind the blocked entrance lies an untouched valley. Imposing mountains protected it from the Fireball, and it remains as the Herd remembers it, green and magical. The lake sparkles crystal clear, and the trees teem with birds. These are the Nesting Grounds where the Herd traditionally lays its eggs. It is, as Eema says, "the most beautiful place there is!"

Aladar leads the Herd, blinking and amazed, out of the cave. Many of them had started wondering whether the Nesting Grounds even existed anymore.

Loving New Family

Aladar and the lemurs have two new family members—Neera, and a little hatchling, who looks just like his dad! Aladar's unique, inter-

species family symbolizes the Herd's new era of tolerance, community, and love.

THE HERO

Aladar's triumph makes him the hero of his age. He has fulfilled his destiny, as a leader and a father. The outsider who taught the Herd a new way of living and delivered it from extinction has earned his prize—a peaceful home...and Neera's love.

Baylene

Strong, enclosing mountains

Eema

Child iguanodon

Pool Party

The whole valley has a festival atmosphere as the Herd heads for the lake. After weeks of scorching desert, this is no mirage, but a desire fulfilled, a dream come true. A flock of birds, gliding on warm air currents, performs a victory fly-by over the triumphant parade.

MIGRATION

• Many dinosaurs join migratory herds in order to reach their habitual nesting grounds in safety. Pterosaurs also travel long distances to mate and breed annually in the same place.

• When the Nesting Grounds become cold in winter, the Herd will head south again for warmer weather.

Dreamy clouds *Sunlight dappling the valley* *Joyous bellow*

The lemurs *Nest* *Aladar* *Neera*

Eema and Plio help the dinosaur mothers tend to their eggs and nurse the newborns. Eema is an old hand at these tasks, and Plio is possibly the only lemur in the world with iguanodon baby nursing experience!

The Herd is saved! The valley is now dotted with hundreds of nests, which regenerate and give new life to the Herd. The future is unknown, but thanks to Aladar these magnificent creatures have survived.

New Beginning

Against all the odds, the animals are saved through the bravery of an unusual group of friends. The Nesting Grounds now echo with the cries of joyous parents welcoming their hatchlings to the world, and the Herd is safe from danger and evil in an enclosed valley. Here children play happily in the warm, nurturing sun; dinosaurs of all species congregate peacefully around the lake and feast on the plentiful leaves, and life goes on and on...

Dorling Kindersley

LONDON, NEW YORK, SYDNEY, DELHI, MUNICH,
PARIS, and JOHANNESBURG.

PROJECT EDITOR David John

PROJECT ART EDITOR Robert Perry

DESIGNERS Guy Harvey & Kim Browne

MANAGING EDITOR Karen Dolan

MANAGING ART EDITOR Cathy Tincknell

US EDITOR Gary Werner

DTP DESIGNER Jill Bunyan

PRODUCTION Jo Rooke

Published in the United States by
Dorling Kindersley Publishing, Inc.
95 Madison Avenue
New York, New York 10016

First American Edition, 2000

2 4 6 8 10 9 7 5 3 1

Library of Congress Cataloging-in-Publication Data

Dinosaur: the essential guide.-- 1st American ed.
p.cm
ISBN 0-7894-5452-1
1. Dinosaurs--Handbooks, manuals, etc.

QE862.D5 D415 2000
567.9--dc21
                                                    99-086291

Reproduced by Colourpath, England
Printed and bound by L. Rex, China

Dorling Kindersley would like to thank:
Eric Huang, Hunter Heller, Victoria Saxon, Rachel Alor,
Brent Ford, and Tim Lewis at Disney Publishing;
Pam Marsden, Eric Leighton, Ralph Zondag,
Cristy Maltese, and most especially Serge Riou at
Walt Disney Feature Animation.

For our complete catalog visit

www.dk.com